Buying this book or downloading it you donate 50 cents to the IHP association for the health and the safety of all the mistreated horses:

http://www.horseprotection.it

On their side

Humans don't always learn easily what respect for life is. They don't consider other animals as companions with which to cohabit, but like things to use and throw away afterwards. Horses, more than other species, suffer from this culture, which has little that is natural and a lot that is anthropocentric. A horse is hardly considered a friend, because he is always a horse "to do something": trotting horse, racing horse, jumping horse, dressage horse, riding school horse, carriage horse, circus horse…slaughtering horse: the same terminology underlines that he doesn't exist as an individual in the average consideration, but only on his utility. He doesn't have rights. IHP was born to encourage a change and to shake consciences: it is our solemn commitment to equines, who make us better persons with their gentleness, their depth and their pride.

THANKS!

I dedicate this book to Christine Contilli, my traveling companion!

WWW.SAMILLA.WORDPRESS.COM

WWW.CATASTINISAMANTA.ILCANNOCCHIALE.IT

MOUNTAIN AIR

CATASTINI SAMANTA

www.samilla.wordpress.com

FLORENCE-BOLZANO

August 2008

I knew that it was not easy to abandon my city and go elsewhere, but it was what I needed. It's not pleasant to live in the smog and bustle everyday, the person feels more familiar to end the need to look a bit of peace. And I own that I needed. A place where silence reigned supreme. Trentino. That was my goal! Far from the noise, stress from parking... Alberto. Yes, why not just running away from life as always, but also a love story gone wrong. I continued to put all my hopes on the wrong men and promptly opened a new wound in my heart and in my esteem. It was time to turn the page and think a little to myself, leaving everything behind me. Forever. I was going to put all the expensive seats from my psychology. I fell alone, but also I didn't want to think. Freedom to go out with an old suit and his hair uncombed, without being looked at as a beggar. Not seeing the same people who reminded me of my ex-boyfriend. No more stumbling in places frequented by him and his boring friends. So in two words I wanted to escape. Without thinking much about, I chose a real estate agency to entrust the sale of my studio. In less than a week I had already found two possible buyers. Naturally I opted for those willing to pay more for my dear four walls. I tried not to look at what I was leaving because it was just heartbreaking and I would have recorded on my feet. I struggled to pay for the damn mortgage, but it was worth it. Apartments in Florence cost a lot and I became one of those. Every now and then a stroke of luck does not hurt. With what I had pocketed could buy me a new, three times as large. At least my two cats would have more room for their night raids. Salt, pepper and white as snow, gray ash, were my family. When I returned home I found them crouching behind the door waiting in quivering. I just threw it on the couch exhausted fought the place at my side. I warmed my feet at night and I rocked with their purring. So were a fundamental part of my life. My work involved saw them again. I was doing the freelance graphic design for some publishers, in short I created the covers of their books. Work comfortably at home with my laptop. Salt and Pepper watched spellbound the keyboard and the cursor moved quickly on the screen until the view to catch him, had thrown on the ground all my papers, let them play quietly then I was forced to make a cry for restore calm on my desk and in my brain. They were my biggest concern for the long journey that we should take with my poor old Twingo. I went exploring a few weeks earlier, in late August to select the house to buy. For that occasion I had to call a Dogsitter, in which case we should say, classifieds, care for my two pests. It was torture because I had done everything in a hurry for fear of suffering from my absence. In less than one day I found the small town where I found my inner peace. It was perched on the mountains surrounding Bolzano. The unspoiled nature reigned. The center was small, very clean and tidy. Passed very few cars and the air was so nice that seemed to dream. Cows and sheep were scattered on either side of the road and the houses with their roofs brown, silhouetted against a sky so clear and blue to look like retouched with a computer graphics program. As soon as I closed the door of my poor car, I had given myself a pinch on the cheek. Could exist a place in the world? Because I had not noticed before? A small and fleeting uncertainty had hit me when I noticed a billboard for the winter skiing. Then I smile, it would certainly be my aversion to the sport to give me that splendid vision. Luck continued to be my friend because I just found a nice apartment in the center, in front of the post office, a room that is used as a post office, large and comfortable. It had two bedrooms, large living room with kitchenette, a beautiful brick fireplace and a bathroom with shower and bathtub. The icing on the cake were two spacious terraces on which my cats would be kept under control throughout the neighborhood. Before leaving this town I stopped in a small furniture shop. Within an hour I had chosen a blue painted wooden bed with matching bedside tables and a large wardrobe of the same color, kitchen pink, two white leather sofas, some libraries and a bathroom vanity. I gave a deposit and was mounted in the car to take the grueling trip home. Now I can not go back, it was decided, that is my new country! Florence was waiting for me with her captivating beauty but this time I was touched. I was furious and had decided to leave. The only news which I unexpected was to find my own Alberto in front of the door.

"Selvaggia, where did you finish? Two days of intercom and I've never found."

"I returned homesick? Or better than that would also be home."

"What are you going to do? They told me that you sold the studio. Where do you want to go?"

I was trying to enter, but he still put in between. It was beautiful as always. Perfumed and well dressed. His blue eyes pierced my soul, but I never sold. I must be strong and remember all the harm I had done. Months had promised me to come live with me then, exactly at the appropriate time, he always found an excuse. Friends had primacy over everything and then even on me. Surely I had never loved. Or at least not what I had loved him, otherwise he would have left his clothes in my closet for some time. He could be sweet as fleeting and my heart was consumed in waiting exhausting. Risk of loss in a vicious circle from which there would be more outgoing. The time had come for decisions and with someone like him I just made a bad choice.

Alberto, please don't recite the story of all time, this time I don't believe it! I sold the house and childbirth week. Destination unknown! At least for you. I never want to see or hear."

"Love, but how do I live without you? You know you're the most important person in my life."

I could have sworn that he tried to recite those words in front of a mirror. He was also unconvincing in himself, let alone persuaded me again.

"Forget! Not be difficult. Farewell!"

I had closed the door in his face. I was due to sit on the first stairs condo not to faint. I can do it, sure I can do to live without him. I just have to convince me! I tried to remember the techniques of yoga to stay calm and I repeated that I was doing the right thing. We thought through. But I knew that I had no way out. If I wanted to live as a coward and rubbing worm I get on that damn machine and come back to that sort of earthly paradise. Luckily I had signed the contract for a house and paid half of the furniture or I just know that I opened that door and.... everything would be back to normal, especially Alberto. Salt and Pepper waiting for me behind the door.

When I entered, I thrown at my feet and purring, rubbing my legs were. I had been delighted with the boxes which I buy during the trip.

"These are the new meals. Those who understand the next week."

In my heart I just hope that that moment came as soon as possible. They say that starting is a bit of death means for me to start living again. Or at least try. The days went by fast and boxes of work to prepare. Albert phoned me at least three times a day. He never answered even when attacked on the intercom. Now I know that men are fascinated by what they can not get. And I now appear unattainable. But, when I was new and concrete again, I lost my fascination passenger. I decided not to greet anyone. Only my various employers were aware of my change of residence. It didn't touch me in any way so the way my work is not changed. All e-mail! Benedict computer! My life!

The ride to Bolzano was a nightmare. I was also able to sell my old car and buy a new Twingo at a reasonable price. It was as if, with the latter, I had cleaned all the past uncomfortable that I wanted to forget. Now I had little to me back. Except the heart, in spite of myself, occasionally, if not often, returning from Alberto. That road seemed endless. Salt and Pepper had been good and quiet but I was still stopped many times in places of service and isolated, with two leashes for cats, I tried to amuse them. Or better to avoid them to leave their needs in my new car. I was really ridiculous! Especially because they were not completely used to being controlled and attempted, with all their strength, take off the collar. The phone kept ringing, careless driving with classical music in the background, precisely Mozart. After facing the tight turns that led to my paradise, I breathed a sigh of relief. Now I began a new life. Would not it be easier to live in a place so far away from all my loved ones but the fact of having decided to make me feel safe as I had never been before. Even Alberto, with all his phone calls, study desk, I would change my mind. Salt and pepper, just released, had been rushed to the white leather sofa that had given me during my absence. I left the keys to the controller furniture store that had taken care to assemble all the furniture that I choose. The result was more enjoyable than I thought. The house was cozy and youthful. I had been given the feeling of family as if we had always lived. I made several trips up the stairs, being the third floor, with all the boxes full of clothes and utensils. When I almost finished the grueling marathon and I found a girl waiting for my front door.

"Hello, you're the new tenant?"

"Yes Hello. I have just arrived. Excuse me for my confusion."

"My name is Rosa. Do you need help?

"Selvaggia. Nice to meet you. No, I think that I ended up traveling. Sign we can offer a quick coffee. Time to put the mocha on fire so we do two words and we know it."

I was afraid and then just closed the door behind her, I began to look around.

"But that nice! It’s 'very hospitable. And especially as youthful style.”

"Thank you! Thinking that it took me an hour to choose is not all that bad."

I had given a chair to sit on and then I started to fill the coffee maker. That girl inspired me with confidence. He had large dark eyes, a translucent complexion and blonde hair with a bob cut short, the classic image of Alto Adige. She seemed sincere, her interest didn’t seem driven only by curiosity, but also by a deep desire to find a new companion. I noticed that the country was populated mostly by adults or older. Maybe she represented a breath of fresh air. Rosa, for me, had arrived at the right time and I would have done by Cicero in this new universe. We would have enriched each other.

"Why did you come to live here? Do you know someone? "

"No. None. You're the first person to talk to. Except the real estate agent and the furniture.
I looked puzzled. The coffee in my cup was definitely cooling while Rosa was trying to understand why a girl suddenly abandoned Tuscan had a wonderful city like Florence to finish in a village, among the wolves and forgotten by God seemed to me that what I was going to request is permissible in view of my condition, had not anything malicious, just a curiosity. I too would his own questions to a newcomer.

"The confusion of the city I was close with it and I had a love story behind that was eating me... say that I came to take a healthy breath of fresh air!"

"Here you have so much peace to regret even the smog!"

"So I chose my destination well. And you? Were you born here?"

"Basically, the farthest I visited Bolzano where I graduated in modern literature and where I work as a teacher in a middle school. Sometimes I would run away from here but I know I would not do ever. Here is my life, my affections. I admire you for your courageous choice. I couldn't have ever done."

I was sitting, exhausted, in front of her. The steaming coffee in my cup. I decide not to drink the last minute because I had not remembered to get milk. For me, a serious failure since I don't add any sugar. Without showing it I had eaten in one go just as you would with a syrup for the flu. Rosa seemed not to have noticed because she was cuddling Pepper, since she went home, she did nothing but she was rubbing her legs.

"Sometimes you have to make decisions for their own good even if it seems you to go away from your everyday life. We say that is a gamble with fate. Or a challenge. Overturn the rules we are used to create new ones."

"But I think there is something very specific that arises such a decision. Everything has a reason."

"And because love moves the universe, if my love I only created pain and problems, I could only escape."

Rosa smiled, looked more relaxed and at ease in my apartment full of boxes yet to open.

"What do you do? Something that allows you to work from home?"

"Yes, I design covers for small publishers and books intended primarily for children."

We continued talking for another half an hour later to greet me when I had made the proposal that was waiting anxiously.

"I sometimes go out together? Here we do not do anything special except go to some pub or restaurant."

"Perfect! Thanks, I'd be happy. You will be my guide for these bristling necks!"

When I closed the door I was thrown on the couch exhausted. To this day I had my small victory. I was not entirely alone.

Within a week I had found my pace. I got up early and after settling the house, cared for my two pests and made a healthy and hearty breakfast, I slipped a plush jumpsuit and went to take a nice walk lasting an hour or so. Enjoy every inch of the road trod, I admired the green fields and snowy mountains in the background. I like living in a painting every day and discovered a new path forward. The air was fresh and pure and filled the only gap in the landscape of that place, the reluctance of residents to welcome the stranger. The language was an insurmountable barrier for me. I studied German in high school but after graduation exam I had abandoned him and quickly forgotten. In my university course I opted for French and Spanish so now those sounds seemed to come from a world far away. A few words I could pick but took too long to understand the correct meaning because, as I discovered later, was an Austrian. For me it was a big obstacle to overcome. Fortunately, younger people spoke Italian well enough, otherwise I would have sunk into a sad silence. I could not do anything, that language is not entered my head. I found her cold and expressionless. Even the sweetest phrase seemed a serious reproach. In my heart I knew that I would never have learned. I studied German for years and not remember a word. Before returning home and start work on the computer I stop and only the small supermarket in the main square of the village. He was my world of temptation. I would get lost among those small and narrow shelves where teas, chocolate and jams reigned supreme. Every day I let groped by a different taste and then I stopped to admire the fruit and vegetables in their wicker baskets overflowing. Invariably I bought colorful salad that tasted enriching them with giant olives and goat cheese into chunks. I felt like Alice in Wonderland, especially when I passed the small, but provided, refrigerator, where the bacon dumplings I looked inviting. And I gave in on time. When I returned home, just steps from the shop, I realized that walking was completely frustrated with food just purchased. In any case it was a remedy for the lungs and eyes. Salt and Pepper claimed, with great leaps and merged, their morning ration of pampering. Just leaned the shopping bags on the floor with his head flung themselves to their internal browser with the hope of finding something for them. To avoid that poured all the contents outside distracted them with some pieces of raw meat. After fixing the purchases in their rightful place in the kitchen, I finally sat down at my workstation. So I spent three hours uninterrupted graphics creation, provided that the two pests let me. In fact you place one on the left side to the other computer to jump right on the keyboard to chase my hands first and then the cursor on the screen. Initially rebuked them and drove them away, but the scene was so funny, I been affected by their playfulness. I did roll the pen on the table and chasing them like crazy. In an instant I arrived at lunchtime and after a quick but hearty meal, I am delighted with another short walk. During one of these outputs afternoon I realized that the Grand Hotel, located in the main square, out of yoga courses. It was my favorite sport and I thought I was dreaming when I saw that poster hanging on the door. I was hesitant in the entry hall where a thin and very pretty girl I had met with kindness. After I explained that the course was open to everyone, not just to hotel guests, had given me a sheet with the times and, without thinking twice, I had just entered. On the way back home I thought everything was going better than I imagined. And, strangely, not even felt the lack of Alberto. I thought every day, but I had put an end to our story. And the distance was really the best choice I ever made in my life. Maybe I can grab the reins of my life!

I would wake up and look in the mirror with pleasure. Although I still looked sleepy picture of me that I saw was very different from what I used to see. My cheeks had taken on a pinkish color, I no longer had the classic dark circles due to sleepless nights, and my big brown eyes had acquired a new light. Even the hair of a black rebels were brighter and healthier. I had to admit that this sudden change of life, but above all, had given me only improvements. I jumped to hear the bell that sounded repeatedly. Eight in the morning who could never be at that hour?

"Selvaggia, are you awake?"

Rosa was calling me from behind the door. I never thought twice about opening them. Would not have noticed in my pajamas or full of childish doodles in my slippers in the shape of a cat.

"Hello! What do you bring on this hour?"

I had never seen her so well dressed. She wore a black suit that made her very professional. With one hand holding a folder with photocopies inside.

"I was going to Bolzano by bus to get to school, and since not return home till late afternoon, I wanted to know if you come with me tonight for a pizza."

"Of course! Today is a day of full-time, this afternoon I have my first yoga class tonight and a nice dinner out there is just fine. Otherwise I would end soon as the chickens to bed!"

"Good. Then step to get you at half past seven. I recommend comfortable clothes because I had thought of going to a restaurant to the country below to not get in town."

"Ok, then I will dress a jeans and a sweater?"

"Sure! There are also my friends."

I finally met some of his own age. This girl is a gift from heaven, and as such it must be ensured. Before leaving I tried something warm to wear in the closet. It was only mid-October and already it was very cold. The locals said that he would soon snowed because the highest peaks were already completely white. After doing my daily walk, coming home I noticed that Pepper was limping. In closing the terrace I had noticed that a vase of flowers had fallen in the garden. I was a suspect immediately jumped to mind. He bent too far forward on the railing of the iron railing? In this case he really had to be still alive. A flight from the third floor was not a trivial matter. I had picked up to check if he had any wound but he started meowing desperately. I could not wait until the pain passed. It took just a snapshot. I settled quickly and I was spending directly from newspaper to ask if he knew a veterinary clinic equipped. I thought I would have given one to Bolzano and rather to my surprise, I had said that the country stood a very advanced center.

"Miss, he is the best doctors in the entire region. I remain satisfied with their performance. They love animals very much that care. Not like some vets who think only of money! Don't make me talk!"

I had hardly realized that every word was followed by an Italian South Tyrol. He was nevertheless able to convince me and, since there was no time to lose, I took the cage in the garage and I live in the house was to catch the person. At the sight of salt cage began to mew and worried when he realized that was not to him but his brother, tears and he had become desperate. I don't you ever shared. Embracing slept, ate in the same bowl, practically living in symbiosis. How could I explain that the distance would only last the time of the visit? Within minutes I had reached to the study. To my surprise the waiting room, though it was the lunch time, it was full of people. I was struck by the scent of flowers, unusual in a place full of animals. Cleaning the floor and chairs were impressive. Indeed shops, businesses and the same streets that I had attended until then were so polished and ordered to cause the greatest respect. I had never thrown a chewing gum on the floor or even a paper towel. Action applicant in my city where almost no one took any notice of where he was going. Three small dogs were sniffing the cage while Pepper blew afraid. I noticed two plaques hanging at the entrance. "Dottori Pontini Giorgio e Waicher Walter."

As the patients came with their owners diminished my initial fear. That place gives me peace, I felt that my little fever was in safe hands. The walls were covered with drawings a bit naive depicting grazing animals, horses, dogs, cats and rabbits. The central table was not only full of magazines, but were also novels of a famous publishing house. I was going to pick one to pass the time when the door was wide open and a man with a white coat I had mentioned to enter. I was in the grip of a hallucination? Raoul Bova was what I was smiling? The vet had noticed my momentary absence and tried to wake up.

"Excuse me young lady wants to get in? I do not see anyone after her patient! "

In addition also had a Tuscan accent. I was not sure I could be wrong, I would have recognized as much.

"Yes I'm sorry I was distracted."

I got up and was also to leave the cage and Pepper on a chair beside me, when I noticed the look of the veterinarian in that direction. I was quick to raise my poor cat, who by then had stopped meowing, and I entered the room visits.

"Pleased to meet the doctor Pontini. What happened to this beautiful cat?"

His voice was warm and calm. The large and powerful hands, slightly tanned and two brown eyes that mirror.

"Nice to meet you. My name is Selvaggia Mazzini and I arrived a little over a month here. I have two cats, brothers, and this morning, when I came home, I noticed that Pepper was limping."

I was watching carefully. The cat didn't seem afraid, but when the pressure on the offending leg had made a mewing desperately that I had torn my heart.

"He has no idea if it fell from somewhere. The cats like to climb and, at times, may lose their balance."

I had reported seeing the vase of flowers on the ground in the garden. The words came out slow and I felt my face burning. But that is silly? These reactions have only during adolescence! But I'd love to be me instead of Pepper! And maybe take away that white coat!

"I think it has nothing broken, but to be sure I prefer to do an X-ray. I can follow in the next room? I need your help to hold it."

I followed him dazed. He had a fresh scent that I liked to be crazy. I could neither speak nor ask questions. My throat was dry and cold hands, even frozen emotion. I almost felt like when I was about to take an oral exam at the university, outside the world. Then curiosity got the better had this terrible state when I was falling. "Excuse me for asking, but are you Tuscan?"

"Yes Like you, I think. I'm originally from Fiesole. A quaint village perched above the city of Florence."

I laughed so from taste to finally return to me.

"Look, I'll find a Florentine right here among wolves! I thought of being alone."

"It's a small world."

Even the vet was nice smile. But then the commitment to support the poor Pepper was more difficult than expected, and together we tried to calm him. The outcome of ultrasound had removed all doubt. Pepper was only a bad sprain. I was prescribed some homeopathic medicines and had a small bandage to hold the leg. When I closed the study door I breathed a sigh of relief. The man was really a natural temptation. So nice to look like a dream! I swore to myself that if my fever was cured I would never set foot in quell'ambulatorio. Who knows how many women had at his feet. That's why the waiting room was full of women and more! Enough! I could not do unrealistic fantasies and then I was done with love and men. With my luck in that field it's better for me to watch other shores. After having withdrawn medication in the pharmacy I was locked in the house dedicated to the care of my poor injured. Salt jumped to my feet and happy when I opened the cage began to lick his brother with affection. I was thrown on the couch exhausted. Determined to stand for an hour before I lost some time at work. The yoga class is definitely missed, but not dinner, I could not refuse a last minute. And I would not even have to sleep. I dreamed that handsome young doctor that I lay on the floor of his studio... And you can imagine the rest.

"Selvaggia, are you ready? Don't take the car's keys, we will go with mine. Both the pizzeria is not far from here."

Rosa was waiting for me on the landing of the building. She wore faded jeans and a sweatshirt, just like me. From clothing is immediately sensed that we were not hunting for men. Outside it was very cold in recent days the temperature was much lowered. Sometimes I wondered for that reason I had chosen the Trentino as my residence, I loved skiing, in fact, I was almost annoyed. My parents were obliged to do so when I was little and I fell so many times, still remembered the pain. The idea of spending the last year in the mountains fascinated me, but after the first day, everything turned into a nightmare. I woke in the grip of the nerves, the very idea of those bundled with thermal suits me feel ridiculous. If you were served to absorb the knocks on the floor! Anyway I liked the mountains, I loved watching the snow coming down slowly. The landscape became fabulous, immaculate and for me, strangely welcoming.
"Here, we will come! My cousins and Ines are already seated at the table. Come on! "

The restaurant was very nice. It had a large room with large windows you can admire the wonderful panorama. "Selvaggia, those are Ines, Tomas and Franz!"

The girl was very beautiful. She had green eyes that lit up her ethereal complexion and long blond hair tied in a queue. Franz, her boyfriend, a German seemed to cool features. She mentioned a shy smile.

Tomas, however, looked playful and he was outgoing. "What do you do?"

Ines had one trivial question, but useful to start a conversation that broke the ice between us.

"I am a graphic editorial. Who design book covers."

"That's great! You break our monotony. We are all farmers, peasants alternative word to say!"

That girl was really nice and seemed to have no malice in his eyes. "I think it's very nice to deal with land and livestock. From my part, unfortunately, young people are no longer interested in doing. And the oldest profession and, ultimately, what allows us to live. How would we do without fruit or vegetables? Not to mention the meat, which I omit because they always love to eat."

"Luckily we are in a pizza!"

Tomas had that line to help me because Franz seemed determined not to open his mouth.

"Why did you come here? Florence is a great city. My parents took us when I was little and I'd go back. It's full of monuments!"

Ines talking and gesturing. Every now and then looked at her boyfriend who went on eating without looking up from his plate. "I love the mountains and I hit this place for its tranquility. I'd had more smog and confusion."

I was evasive, but I think that answer had partly satisfied. "You're right I could never live in a big city."

The pizza was very good and the dinner I had advised with Rosa an apple strudel. I had never tasted a cake so inviting and pleasantly

spicy.
"We just opened a farm in our barn, you might consider a logo for the posters and fliers for distribution to do some advertising?"

I looked up to make sure that Franz had been talking. He smiled slightly, but the fact that I had asked for help was a good sign. Outside, meanwhile, it started to snow.

The yoga teacher was a lady of a certain age, agile and flexible as a child. Her face reflected the inner peace. Being in that room full of fragrant incense and lit only by candles, I plunged into a state of infinite calm. When, after an hour and a quarter of lessons, I had to get up and go I did a little of regret. But the fate had made me a beautiful gift to have that opportunity at my hand. Moreover, the lessons took place every day and I had to exercise some force on my instinct not to follow him at all. What would they think if I had presented each evening at six o'clock fitted my blanket and pillow? I could not make me some problems, because otherwise I'd changed cities and way of life? I paid an extra fee then I decided each day, according to mood and commitments, whether to follow the course or not! If you loved so much to do yoga because I had to deprive myself? Only fear being judged, and what then? Another psychological obstacle to overcome: always I give a damn about what others I may think! I was absorbed in these thoughts when, walking with his head down in an attempt to close the jacket, I bumped into a person. Not really any!

"Oh excuse me, but I was careless..."

The rest of the sentence was dead in my mouth. The nice vet the day before he smiled, now he amused. I should just be a good show, hair tousled, face burning in shame certainly throws and pillow and balanced on my arm.

"Good evening, Miss Mazzini. How is your Pepper?"

I could not answer, can not only remember my name, but also the name of my cat? I had to say something or would have thought that there was much head.

"He's much better. The medication alleviated the pain. Just try to take off the bandage but otherwise seems in the process of recovery."

"Good. Don't forget to go for a check in fifteen days. But, do you need a ride? Outside it's snowing strong."

I was taken aback, that I did not expect his kindness. And I also swore to myself that I would never live in that study not to die behind a man who would never have calculated. What was I supposed to answer now?

"I live very close to this. I could get there by myself but I didn't take the umbrella... If you don't mind that I enjoy it."

"Why should he feel sorry? I've been to her proposal. I would say that it's better for you to give us of this point."

He has a disarming beauty. High and mighty. He looked strong but not cold or unfriendly. He could put people at ease.

"Of course. I find it easy to give of herself. I don't do either with my employers."

I had opened the door of the hotel and, with one hand I was holding the umbrella for me not to bathe. We had entered the race in his panda and he quickly warming had access to span the glass.

"And what do you do?"

"I am a freelance graphic, working for some publishers.

"It means that designs the covers?"

"Yes Put simply it. Sometimes even billboards, but also in the literary field."

"Interesting. Too bad I just did achieve our logo, otherwise you would be the right person."

We were getting closer to my house. The curiosity to know what he was doing in that hotel was too strong and, upon reflection a few seconds, I had thought that there was no harm in asking.

"Do you also frequent the yoga's classes?"

"No, I though I'd start. It fascinates me as a discipline. I came to have a sauna to relax. This morning I ran three interventions. And, although I should not, I always emotionally involving. I should not do this job. I can not leave my heart in silence, but sometimes we should be more brain!"

I watched him drive. I felt inadequate to the situation but I had to do something to repay his kindness. We had arrived just in my house when, with the help of do not know which saint, I had suddenly decided to invite him to dinner.

"Do you want to stay and eat something from me? At least you would have also way to check for Pepper the bandage. "

I had not realized what I was clutching a backpack in his hands, but the sudden pain of a nail he had brought to reality. Giorgio turned and he looked at me in silence.

"If you do not willingly accept disorder. I had not yet done shopping and I would direct to buy something already cooked."

"Don't expect a banquet of honor. If you must light the fireplace so I make some pizzas and focaccia."

"Wonderful idea! It's a life that I don't eat a pizza cooked in a wood."

My legs were shaking like a child on his first day of school. His enthusiasm made me happy, but I was scared of failing even to knead the flour. As he closed the car admiring his back lending. He had an athletic body, in a way very similar to Alberto, but his face was something indescribable. He has a disarming beauty, as equals by Raoul Bova put me in awe. For once I think of all possible women's achievements, but to enjoy this unexpected event. I just had to try to behave as I would with any friend. While introducing the key in the lock of the door I took my phone to ring. I stopped and I opened the door to see who was looking for me. Alberto? Without thinking twice I had refused the call. He was the last person with whom I wanted to speak that evening.

"You can respond calmly. I will not be a hindrance."

"No, my friend that when calls would not stop to tell all his amorous adventures. Boring! Please enter as well and supports his jacket and backpack beside the sofa."

He had looked around curiously before becoming the target of Salt and Pepper. They started rubbing her legs fused emitting unabated. I had never seen so affectionate toward a stranger. Yet he was a vet! The same Pepper seemed to have forgotten the bad experience the day before.

"I see you have two cats. They are brothers?"

"Yes I took them when they were little more than two months. I found them in a disused factory. I don't feel like bringing them into a cat shelter. Thei are weak when I comes with the animals. I admit it!"

"It's a good thing. I believe that animal lovers have a strong feeling that him away from any negative feelings toward the human being also. The problem presents itself to someone who gives large effusions for newborns and then maybe leave a dog in the street or mistreats a cat. Well, forget this speech otherwise we enter a minefield... Rather, I congratulate you because you have a very nice apartment. It 'friendly and colorful."

"Thanks. As soon as the agent he asked me because I didn't think twice. Compared to the studio which I had in Florence, this is a palace!"

He began tinkering in the wood in the basket near the fireplace. He seemed at ease and I engage in appearance as peacefully as possible. Who knows how many women wanted to be in my place!

"I guess with what you have gained from that sale have bought this house in peace."

"Actually I was even money to change the car. I think Florence is one of the most expensive cities of Italy. "

"To say nothing of-Fiesole, where if you have a villa overlooking the city are a bastard. If you for a lighter?"

I opened a kitchen drawer looking for him, Giorgio had approached, and when I passed the object of his request, there was a light touch. Our hands for a moment he had touched. I think my face was burning so I had been pretending to be turned in search of flour, just waiting for me on the shelf in front of my face. I seemed to be in the grip of Bridget Jones syndrome. Oh, I had to leave soon. So when he lit the fireplace, I had begun to mix with commitment. If only my parents had instilled a bit of confidence in myself. During my childhood and my adolescence I had only received warnings. My friends were always more talented than me, more beautiful, more educated, in fact I was the only black sheep. And that I always felt in life. When I graduated I had earned a day of glory then they started to want to plan for the future. All work was better than what I wanted to do. Finally, after having had the courage to follow a path of psychological help, I went to live alone. Certainly I don't know that Alberto had done nothing but cast us deeper into the abyss. I had loved with all my heart, but in response, had managed to make me feel misunderstood again. To say nothing of his friends, men and women whose main purpose was to buy the latest phone out on the market or the chief signed the most popular at the moment. For me it was an indescribable torture so often preferred to invent an excuse to stay home wrapped in my pajamas naïve. When we had to go out to dinner I spent hours in front of the cupboard and I wear whatever I felt out of place anyway. The girls were walking casual in their ten centimeters high heels while I was reeling with half heel boots. It was not a pastime but a torture. Yawned in front of their fervent discussions about buying clothes or favorite places to spend your next holiday. I felt guilty. I always thought that I was the wrong one. And with this conviction continued to bend to the will of Albert. Unfriendly man, too busy on himself by noticing my needs.

"Why did you decide to come in Trentino? Also if I can ask it."

Giorgio had offered to set and was arranging the dishes with an almost maniacal attention. That question was more than legally. I just had to answer as best as possible, ie with absolute sincerity.

"If I told you that I have chosen the vicinity of Bolzano only my innate passion for the mountains, but skiing, You don't take me seriously. So I just have to get you the most shameless confession. I ran away from a city which I adore, even if he was choking, as the story with my ex-lover."

"He was on the phone, first?"

"Yes But not as you think. I don't run away from him because I did suffer or had betrayed me, but only because I did not feel appreciated for what they really are. Or rather I didn't feel accepted. "

"Welcome to Paradise!"

That answer I was shocked, I didn't understand if you were making fun of me and if so, why. Maybe I was watching open-mouthed as he sat on the couch and he smiled slyly.

"I'm not kidding. This place has the power to bring peace to the heart or head. According to our needs. I came away from Fiesole because I felt inadequate in my hometown, and when my sister married a guy Brixen not think I've got twice the reach. Here I would take care of other animals not just dogs and cats. And my most important dream was to live surrounded by nature, I wanted to drown. And never return back, I'm happy with the choice made because of graduation. We ate with the help of two old friends. Giorgio told me his university curriculum. His internship in a Florentine studio and nightclubs that had attended. We both marveled'd never encountered one another since we had the same passion for the theater. I spent two hours in absolute peace. Moreover, the pizza came so well, why I was able to do. After the first half hour of embarrassment I felt like I was relieved to have found such a person like me in tastes and behavior. For a moment I touched the idea of the myth of the half, that Plato was able to describe with such skill as to lead any living being to its exhausting research. Then I had just awakened. How could a man so attractive to be satisfied with me? That's who started my low self-esteem, that tramandatami parents. In the end they are a beautiful girl, but I can not rely on my good looks for me in the eyes and attitudes all my insecurity. Time to say goodbye to my embarrassment had regained the upper hand. Giorgio had picked up his jacket only after filling of pampering Salt and Pepper that did not stop purring satisfied. I was holding up the door for easy exit when, unexpectedly, I had raised my chin with his right hand to gently kiss her lips. I was so stunned by failing to respond to sudden intimacy. Then I had embraced with enthusiasm and had returned the kiss with all the passion I could muster.

"I'm sorry. I don’t want that you think something badly of me or want to spoil this wonderful evening but I felt the need. I like you and very wild. I never imagined to feel so close to a woman as happened tonight "

I was still holding up the door. A vile and petty attitude as if I wanted to ask to leave my house. I had awakened from the dream because I had heard my thought was unimaginable even brighter. I must have seemed comical, red-faced and silent as a mature pepper.

"Here... I.... I also love me but..."

Giorgio had opened his eyes awaiting the end of my sentence. And I could not find the courage to tell him all, but I had to do.

"But?"

"But, I can never compete with all the girls falling at your feet! You are damn fascinating and beautiful and I don't want to fight a battle already lost."

"What are you saying? It does not seem to have crowds of courtesans behind me! So what should I say you too are a particularly attractive girl therefore I should not declare? I should not hope for our love story because you may have other suitors? This is madness!"

I knew perfectly well that he was right but I was afraid. I did not feel to face a new relationship with the old wounds still heal. I preclude my slice of happiness.

"I don't feel. I'm still shaken my experience... and I lost."

I didn't finish the sentence that was already headed for the stairs.

"I recommend the drugs for Pepper. Must continue to take them for at least a fortnight. Then, if you want, you can always bring the studio to a control. Thanks for the pizza, it was really delicious and ... good night! "

I was not even able to answer that already had walked the three flights of stairs and was opening the door of the apartment building. Good! Nobody beat me in knowing I complicate my life!

I was washed up the dishes when the doorbell had started to play repeatedly. Only Rosa was so insistent and perhaps she was the right person to raise my heart.

"Hey, are eleven at night and if I'm not mistaken has just released a handsome veterinarian from your apartment. Pepper seems in good shape. Who was that “Adone” in your house?"

I was launched on the couch and I took a chocolate from the coffee table. I was in pajamas and slippers. I tossed the dry ground and I broke into tears pouring down. I had told all sitting at his side clutching a handkerchief in her hands.

"How silly you are. Why deprive you of this opportunity only for the fear of failure? Not suffer equally the idea of not experience love? How can you assume another failure? Giorgio gets some blame for its beauty. What do you suggest that all people are handsome surface and brought to the betrayal by nature?"

In my heart I knew that she was right, but a mysterious force made me reject the idea of a new romance. Lately I had become accustomed to my loneliness.

"Rosa can’t do it. There's something inside me which tells me not to be ready. I'm afraid I might fall in love without reservation and suffer no escape. I have yet to heal the wounds that left me the link to Alberto, I throw myself into the arms of another! "

"For me you are wrong. I respect your choice, but I must also tell you to stop crying, it makes no sense! "

She was right: I was acting like a silly girl. I made a decision, however painful it was, I had to take him forward with dignity. To begin with I had to find another vet. I could review Giorgio. I could not face him.

But not everything goes as you want or rather, if the head requires us to behave and heart favors another, we always end up following the second. Even when we know we can run into a new defeat we can not flinch. So I had done before the proposal of Giorgio to accompany him to Bressanone to buy some veterinary products at a wholesale specialist. I had come across him as I entered in the yoga class. He preceded me in the hall and I mentioned to sit next to him.

"What are you doing here?"

"I followed your advice and, instead of making me a sauna, tonight I decided to try this famous relaxed discipline. I hope not to bother you with my presence."

Without waiting for my response, he begun to spread your blanket while I looked dazed. I thought that I had ended any chance of mending our young friendship and instead I showed no sign of trouble for what I had said the night before.

"Hey! Are you going to stand there motionless or teach me something before which reaches the teacher?"

The room was still empty and I felt embarrassed for Giorgio as he was behaving. He treated me like a friend of long standing and that way of doing kept me even more uneasy. I didn't know if he put a brick on top of the little that had happened between us or if it was a tactic to mend a relationship ever started. Maybe it was the time to stop for asking questions that I would not have been answered and to enjoy what the life was offering me.

"I don't that think you can do without this sport once tried".

"Basically, this is which I thought when I wake up this morning remembering the beautiful night we spent together... except your greeting a bit 'grumpy'."

I think that I become in all the colors besides not find the strength nor the words to answer without sounding silly or arrogant. The arrival of other people, and the same teacher, I had taken me from that situation. But only for one hour lesson. Giorgio ran the positions with a mastery that made me suspect that he had done yoga and had made fun of me making me believe otherwise. In comparison I was an amateur but I practiced now the discipline since some years. After the much loved final relaxation (which that day had only helped increase my anxiety), the handsome veterinarian took me to the door of the dressing room for women.

"Congratulations you have been very good. How is the lesson?"

"Best of my expectations! Do you know that I'm no expert on this stretch of I had no difficulty to perform all movements."

I started to laugh out loud while Giorgio looked at me almost angrily.

"I'm sorry but I had almost come to suspect that I had already practiced yoga."

"But you are always so biased with others?"

The question embarrassed me, because he had hit the mark. Actually I always did a mountain of problems on everything and everyone. I was really boring!

"Tomorrow I have the afternoon free. Should I go to withdraw homeopathic products in Bressanone, I wondered if I was going to keep me a company."

"I didn't visit that city and I have all spoken very well. May I take this opportunity to make a tourist, why not?"

I would have never confessed that I would go with him even on the glaciers. Only after I having closed the door of the locker room and I was given the silly. As I still stood in his presence without love?

All morning I was not even able to work. I looked at the computer screen dazed, unable to capitalize on any idea I came into her head. I did nothing but I watch my two pests that are chasing each other like crazy. Pepper seemed to have no more pain in the leg but sometimes he would stop shooting to lick the wrapping compartment intent to remove. After a good hour of complete inactivity, I was wrapped in my warm duvet, and I made a little walk to the village close to buying a newspaper and some new type of tea. (I had a magazine full of kitchen!) I could not feel so upset for an appointment that had no semblance of an encounter of love. I had put into his head that it was nothing, but an afternoon in the company of a new friend, (like a stupid) I was kicked out of my house crashed. I was acting more on impulse and then I regret it in ten, no, in fact, five minutes later. I knew: I did it for fear of suffering, but I had avoided getting lost in her eyes and I fall like a pear cooked at his feet as soon as I saw it. That afternoon it would have been decisive for my heart. Yet I could not give up. What would I wear? A jeans and a sweater, as the day before and the day before. What difference did it make? I could not wear much, I was just dull. I knew that with a skirt or a dress that you could see the curves of my body I seemed Olivia waiting for Popeye. Are not thin, no, my flesh in the right places, but my height makes me almost awkward when I try to get elegant, short dresses or long that I do dress up a broom! Also, do not feel comfortable, they are quite comical and out of place. A colorful sweater all stuck between other more monotonous. I had grabbed a moment without thinking. I like bright colors, though I know what a blue or black are more professional, but do not fit me, confusing and uncertain. Why waste that much time in choosing the clothing when, with the cold and the sky that threatened a new snowfall, we'd been locked up in the nose with our quilts? At the sound of the intercom had entered the panic of a fifteen to his first appointment. I tripped on the carpet of the room and almost had bumped into his head in the door handle. So I would have welcomed with a nice bump on his forehead or even a cut to heal. So it's a vet will be able to operate on people! I became, once again, of silly and I opened the door pretending to be calm light years away from me.

"Hey, all right? I heard a muffled sound coming from the hall."

Here, this has also heard the extra fine! Now what I invent? Fortunately Pepper was nearby and he looked at him curiously, and perhaps even a bit worried about remembering who he was, even if he not accompanied by his terrifying white coat.

"Yes! The two chased each other my pests and they almost got dropped."

"Well! It means that this beautiful cat is recovering faster than I expected."

Salt, who had not yet clearly understood who represented Giorgio for the animal, rubbing her legs fused emitting no end. Pepper, however, was defensive.

"I think that it's better to go before dark. I'm going to make a visit to a farm dedicated to the collection and sale of apples."

"Original! We are in the region of apples!"

Oh but what I said? I always spoke when instead I should just keep quiet and do a big smile. I hid my blushes looking for the bag and down jacket to wear.

"Well. We'll make a trip in Bressanone. I am sure that its characteristics will hole in your heart. "

The Panda of Giorgio seemed to know perfectly that way. I fought every bend if I admire the breathtaking view or close his eyes for fear of flying below. I knew that nature is married perfectly with the city of Bolzano, which loomed in the background as a memory card, but could not overcome my fear that road full of curves. In the end we were down by a small village in the Alps and certainly I could not expect a straight and plain boring!

"Let me understand, are you afraid of the road or of my driving?" Giorgio smiled, amused by my terrified expression and certainly comical.

"I'm doing a pretty picture, right? I don't like the curves and I know it may seem a paradox for a person who has chosen to live almost on top of a mountain. I have to say that I still get used at all."

"I think that as soon as possible if you don't want to lock us in your apartment for the rest of your days... it would be a shame! Do you know what you're missing? Bolzano is exquisite and it offers all kinds of fun. Do you want to have a change from the little village where there are refugees, or am I wrong?"

I didn't responde, but I was limited to looking around, hiding the slight nausea that gripped my poor stomach.

"How many vines! I didn't notice before."

Giorgio made a maneuver some daring to stop at a large farm, which topped the written drawings of white grapes, because of course incomprehensible language Alto Adige, seemed a winery.

"We in advance how about buying a few bottles of white wine a bit sparkling? I know this brand and it's one of the best in the area."

"Why not?"

That afternoon was promising really well. Except my stupid sore machine!

The cellar was well stocked and the wine was of excellent quality. After the first glass I had had to stop to avoid starting to laugh like crazy. In fact I could cope well enough alcohol but I didn't stop laughing at everything that could say to me or it could shown to me. A stupid person almost seemed hopeless! Giorgio, however, continued in his professional tasting exchanging views with the sales staff.

"Is it right if I buy a small box and maybe we will drink a bottle at your house tonight?"

Before I could answer he had supported the glass on a barrel and I had mentioned to wait to open his mouth.

"I swear that I touch even with a finger. Are you controlling the bandage of Pepper?"

How I wish a nice dinner by candlelight including later... but this was just what I had gone to his head...

"Sure, why not? Buy a nice amount of fresh apples and maybe something in Bressanone, and we're horse!"

But with that silly words I had finished the sentence? Perhaps the wine had nevertheless yielded a certain effect. And he, mocking, just laughed at me.

"Umh... I know that we should invite your friends. Otherwise I don't know if I will keep the promise just made it!"

How I wish you not maintained!

"Since we would not even bring myself to stop at the farm."

I had walked into the Panda as the snow began to fall in large flakes. Not even felt the cold, the veterinarian had the power to make me walk on air. I just hope to be able to hide my emotions otherwise are fried!

Finally a bit street, flat! I looked over the peaceful surroundings whilst the snow had the magic power to make everything fabulous. An endless stretch of trees as well as a continuation of our right to the left.

"There are these apples?"

"Yes, there are the eyes, as you can see."

I had avoided adding another and I had enjoyed the sight in silence. Giorgio had stopped in front of a structure that it looked like a greenhouse for plants, but that obviously was not since they were just two people out of large transparent bags crammed with red apples.

"Here, my dear, new gourmet fruit indeed dedicated to the queen of fruit par excellence: the apple!"

He opened the car's door and, like a knight of the past, he tried to repair me with a large colorful umbrella.

"You are a man of his word!"

Within many wicker baskets full of red apples, yellow and green. Virtually all varieties to suit every possible taste. We had bought a bag color unless you have tasted at least two each. Although already out of season harvest tasted delicious, fresh and sweet, almost light years away from those we buy in supermarkets.

"Do you go to the central milk behind here too?"

I didn't know if he was kidding or if he was saying seriously. Just finished down to Bolzano I immediately noticed the huge company on whose roof emblazoned the name of one of the most famous companies of Trentino for the production of milk, yoghurt and dairy products. Those products were difficult to find in Florence, but when

I could find them something more than our own. After nearly three months in that landscape now it was clear to me where it came from that taste delicious, in fact cows grazing lush green grass and breathe clean air, then nature did the rest.

"If we continue like this I think your Panda unable even to climb our steep hill."

Laughing like two teenagers had taken over our road to Brixen. The snow showed no signs of decline and the temperature was dropping fast. The city was really beautiful and fascinating breathtaking. Looked more like a small town where time stopped in favor of its own inhabitants. The houses, one after the other, each with a colorful facade and often painted with pastoral scenes, the streets covered with small pebbles clean. Closing my eyes I could almost imagine finding myself in front of some of the wood elf in the company of their own fairy. So I seemed to live in a magical tale!

"Exceeded my imagination! And for me this beautiful town like something out of a fairytale!"

"It's the same effect on me and I think I'll come often to visit my sister who lives near the center with her husband, two dogs and three cats."

"Umh... I don't' know because it happens, but your sister is already sympathetic to me."

Giorgio began to laugh and, perhaps unwittingly, had taken me by the hand. Initially I was so embarrassed that I almost tried to draw back then I was let go and I was close with all my strength to send "affection". For now, I able so to speak!

"Come with me here wholesale?"

I was tempted to go with him but I preferred to walk alone to clarify a bit ideas.

"If you don't mind walking this distance, I'll join you in ten minutes."

"Perfect!"

I had left my hand and offered his umbrella to shelter posandomi a kiss on the forehead. I was stuck at the entrance of the store as a stupid person. What figure should I make a move otherwise think that is a girl who moves to the first contact. The succession of arches had allowed me to walk without getting wet. I entered a food and I was left enthralled by a piece of bacon that seemed to put on display just for me and a box of dumplings just cooked. Behind me baskets of salad made a fine show as if they were beautiful flower arrangements. I was groped by those left and practically in the shopping bag I need you need for dinner. The wine would do the rest. I am risking but I can't turn back.

"Have you looted a store?"

When Giorgio saw my purchase, he rubbed his hands.

"Tonight we make a fine meal! What about going to visit the cathedral and then go for the car? If the temperature drops still we will find the risk of the frost."

In reaching the exquisite main square, where stands the church of Santa Maria Assunta, I admired the windows of some shops already decorated with Christmas decorations. I could not wait to visit one of the many famous markets for sales of balls and decorated with garlands wrapped wood products. The cloister had me stunned with all those plaques to commemorate both the illustrious ancestors of the poor of the place. That town would become my favorite place for my future purchases.

"Giorgio what do you think of fall? The smell of bacon is spreading throughout the cathedral soon someone will tell me something."

"You're still the same, you worry too much about what others think. In any case it's better to go because I have a bit of hunger."

When I say it I had a wink and, of course, I had become of all colors. Perhaps I had become more red piece of bacon lying helpless at the bottom of my shopping bag.

When he reached my apartment I breathed a sigh of relief. The road took some pieces to the sides ice and I had taken a kind of tachycardia. I tried to hide my fear talking incessantly about everything and everyone. But it was in vain. Giorgio now had learned to know.

"The fear makes you such an effect? Or was it the wine?"

"I can't make it a clean with you! Come on preparing dinner that I can't wait to try these dumplings.

While I was inserting the key in the lock of the door I hear a familiar voice behind me.

"Good evening, Selvaggia."

Rosa was coming home at that time. What should I do I have to invite or not? If I do seem to be afraid to be alone with him if I don't think I'm ready to throw his arms. Giorgio looked at me before opening his mouth as if to seek my consent.

"We were just talking about you. Why did not you call the company and also Tomas, Ines and Franz? We bought food for a regiment! "

"Well I can't... I have just returned and I know not if they have other commitments..."

Muttered in vain looking for some excuse to leave us alone. I had to reassure her that their presence would be welcome instead.

"From at least try to call them! We'd love to spend an evening together. "

Rosa looked at me as if it had not been sure of what she had just come from my lips.

"Things will never be done, we live among wolves, not much choice."

Before the last sentence of Giorgio she was determined and she pulled out her cell phone. The three were not made as much as you pray and had immediately accepted the invitation.

"Give me a shower? Are destroyed, arrive home and you have half an hour."

Salt and Pepper had literally gone mad with happiness to see us fall. Jumping and sniffing my bag especially with the bacon. I tried a large wicker basket filled with apples and aviation and the two pests they had stolen one and raced through the house. I sometimes think I want to be somewhere else, but when I came to this paradise, but do not want to stay here the rest of my days. Giorgio moved into my apartment with an impressive mastery. Wasting no time the fire had been lit using the larger logs. Soon the kitchen and living room were heated and even the cats were napping in their kennels under fire. I was almost climbing up a small ladder to dust off some dishes never used before when I was about to ruin the floor if my vet had not quite preparing to extend his arms.

"But what do you want? You could ask me and I offered to take the damned served..."

I felt his eyes scan every particle of my skin and heat was indecipherable hold of my whole person. I'm still not menopausal.

His hands were still clutching my life and I don't remember how we started kissing with almost animal force. We had found lying on the couch panting when Giorgio had stopped, or rather, had stopped his hands were wandering through my hair.

"What am I doing? Damn! I promised not to touch and see what a fine figure as a sailor I was doing! "

"Well I say the same... I have not pulled back, if it can console you."

We were embarrassed, and neither looked at each other's eyes.

"Come on! Come on that soon will ring Rosa and, if we not even find the table set, we can only think of being out of trouble. "

I had arranged my hair, lost the rubber band that it was supporting them, were abandoned to their rebellious nature and certainly at that moment I could only look at a lion attack. In silence I lay one of the best cloths and washed the blessed service Richard Ginori, a period piece recovered little money in the antiques market of San Lorenzo, as the glasses, a strictly different.

"Do you like the old things?"

"Yes, mostly, I love visiting the various markets in search of objects of the past. When I buy I like to think that someone has enjoyed before me and I think we have the strength to pass something magical... I don't know how to explain it... So I like!"

"How many passions we share together? We seem made for each other. I stop here I don't want you to believe me stupid sycophant that seeks only to obtain a fleeting pleasure from you."

I gave right of reply because he had started to cut the bacon as if to put an end to that speech that it was getting much more complicated than expected. I could not help but admire his athletic shoulders expressing all his masculinity. What am I doing here still like a light pole? At least I have to put water on the fire when otherwise the dumplings will cook? I had not yet finished the salad, peel the bell began to ring wildly.

"Hey, what takes to Rosa?"

Open the door I was almost attacked by barbarian horde. Franz, Tomas, Ines and Rosa had poured over the fireplace in the living room supporting a large tray full of sweets. They were all smiling and joyful as I remembered.

"Finally, the veterinary honor us with your presence! For months we promise to come to dinner in our cottage and instead we only do you visit for vaccines administered to our animals. The arrival of Wild gave a change in your life boring sedentary? "

I looked shocked the author of that sentence make me incapable of reason. Giorgio embraced Franz with affection as she smiled like a child has unwrapped Christmas gifts. And to think that the only time I had seen was too quiet and introverted.

"Women are the movement of the universe. You should know my friend, Ines has revolutionized my existence and she convinced me to open a business that until recently hated first."

Between a laugh and a joke we were seated at table. The evening was spent in merriment and time had flown. How many centuries did not feel especially blessed and so happy for anything in distress?

"Do you remember Giorgio that night to help our Rasamunde to give birth to the fault of ice slammed into a tree you are destroying your golf?"

"The health of the foal was much more important in my scrap car and at least I decided to change it. Now with my Panda four-wheel affront any adversity. Even if someone still can not trust my driving. "

I felt I was taken into account, but instead of getting angry, I started to laugh out loud.

"Yes, Today I was only joking."

I drank too much wine and could not stop laughing. I had not even broken when Giorgio had embraced me before all, forcing me to put her head on his shoulders. With that gesture he didn't stay close to my hosts so many doubts about our relationship, but to me, and many! That gesture what it meant? And such an approach was as blatant a statement... but what? I did not want me to other thoughts, let alone questions. That night I decided to follow my instincts (not to mention heart!). When all were gone I had finished two glasses of wine in a flash, and within minutes, had given their results. He cleared and I laughed, he washed the dishes and laughing, always laughing swept. The vet was amused to watch me. He did not move a finger at me, but he worked to get everything back in order. Now or never! Now I don't know when this train will pass! And so I can only hope for the future and if there will be a future I want to enjoy this. For once in my life I have to take the initiative! In vino veritas!

"Do you want to sleep here tonight?"

I had pulled his shirt and before I answer I started to kiss behind the ear. He had pulled back, indeed, I had raised from the ground and carried in your room. The rest I'll leave you to imagine. When you left it stripped from my trembling hands I was left breathless. His body seemed set in stone. And that night on the stone I had a dream.

When I was awakened Salt and Pepper had invaded the bed with small puppets shaped mouse to hide under the covers. Giorgio was no longer at my side. Initially I thought that I imagined all like a good dreamer as I am, but then the presence of my post-it in form of heart-shaped attached to the table it was the proof that that night was really burning.

"Forgive me if we can not have breakfast together this morning but I have a very delicate operation to a dog that risks paralysis. You look at my house (above the surgery if by chance you do not remember!)

To eat together.

Ps in the kitchen there is a croissant with cream and fresh milk.

Giorgio, the veterinarian."

I could have been so lucky to meet such an Adonis all to myself? Instead of walking it seemed to me to fly. I had a hungry despite the great binge the night before. Only after checking the mail and I made a little clean of the house, I had a long relaxing walk. The bitter cold I had refreshed his mind and given new business ideas. In fact I had to deliver a novel cover for a few days later and I still had not started doing anything. But the snowy landscape made me calm as I had never been. Even my usual “paranoia” about men seem to vanish into thin air. I adopted a new philosophy of life based on eating everything without asking me questions about the future. I could never think a year ago to be here today? Tomorrow is always an unknown factor even when everything seems tailored. I was waiting Giorgio in the surgery now desert. On the road I stopped to purchase a wonderful freshly baked strudel. The smell of baked apples and cinnamon had invaded my small car.

"Just desserts? You're not satisfy? "

"Since I live here in Trentino I do nothing but I taste more and, unfortunately, all good. I don’t want to think about the line so disposed with my long walks."

He embraced and kissed me on forehead with one hand, then, he grasped the envelope containing the cake which is still warm.

"You're so perfect! How many girls would like to have your body! Now I say rightly so... you can trust who is not a lie to take heart."

Now no longer I blushed before his compliments that at times they were very ironic. It was pleasant to her company and was also without any emotional involvement. Giorgio was always cheerful and helpful to anyone, unable to show impatience. A sincere friend to the men and women within a confidant. And not only for his ability to laugh and listen. It's a good fight that I'm going to take, how many girls trying to win? His beauty is objective but the rest is even more precious and difficult to leave to others! I could not just do not think I'd risk being standing by his side. My character was too insecure to not make me all sorts of problems, suitable only to destroy what little was building every day. We had lunch and then quickly throw on your couch, the heat of the fire, pampering without respite. The time to leave had come too quickly, but our occupations call calling us. I kissed him with passion and I had reached my utilitarian without looking back. I felt her eyes on me and I almost stumbled over a mound of snow. The usual clumsy! In the short ride home I had thought that I had not heard Alberto, or rather I had not received phone calls which in the end, I never responded. That he had finally put his soul in peace? So I hope with all myself. Now my heart had taken a different road, they seemed so distant times when I spent whole days crying on the couch for that silly fop. And I even wasting time thinking about it. After a session of a tight labor I was so relaxed during yoga lesson ending almost fall asleep during relaxation. I decided not to call Giorgio not to seem too obsessive. Was Friday evening and I bought something at a supermarket near you and I would enjoyed an old movie on dvd eating junk food. The bar before the Grand Hotel was also pastry and where I could go better to find some typical candy? What strange fate sometimes likes to put in the footsteps of grief light years away from our heads. So I discovered the beautiful veterinarian to sit at a table, somewhat secluded, in front of a beautiful girl of who I could see only the long raven hair and a hand which was holding her.

"Good evening, Miss, what do you want?"

I didn't feel even the guy who tried to speak with a strange Italian accent. I grabbed a pastry and I left the money, certainly more than they should, on the counter hurrying to reach the exit. I don't know if he had seen, but he had no account of either would change the excruciating pain that was gripping my stomach. I seemed to hear his voice behind me, but I had not turned. Stupid, that silly, childish that are asking me again trusted a stranger but especially a man! I climbed the stairs when I was crying like a desperate I hit Rosa and I dropped the folder and all the school books.

"Hey, Selvaggia, what happens?"

"I'm just a girl! I trusted to Giorgio and I just found in the company of a woman in obvious closeness to the bar below."

I continued to sob without help my poor friend who was trying to tidy up her things.

"Come let a moment in my house so you calmly tell what happened. And maybe we can drink some tea together."

I had followed like a robot, not thinking that maybe my two pests had heard my voice and I were waiting behind the door. Be patient my darlings, soon arrive.

"Sit down and try to calm down, otherwise I don't understand what you are telling."

I had told again the scene without stopping to cry as she handed me paper towels that filled with bitter tears.

"Can they ever finish to meet only men unreliable?"

"Listen, Selvaggia, I think I understand who is the person you've seen with Giorgio. If she had blacks long hair should be his former girlfriend. Do not you have ever spoken for fear that you refuse to live and inhibited the beginning of this story. Among them is over by then. A year or maybe more. And he was to leave her..."

"Behold, I knew I saw a flash back, instead I was the fuse that has reignited the dormant love."

Rosa didn't know how to comfort me, because the phone began ringing incessantly.

"It's him. We want to talk. Enough!"

I was about to close the door to stop calling me when she was snatched away.

"Giorgio, hello. She was here but she says that she doesn't want to hear you... I imagined him. I tried to tell her but she had a nervous reaction... "

I had grabbed my hand firmly and leave her. Without being able to lift to avoid confrontation I had put the phone to your ear.

"Selvaggia... Selvaggia, please listen a moment, then decide if you believe me or not. I never told about Carla because there was time but because our history is long over and there is absolutely nothing between us... "

"Yes... definitely... tell all so early. Not expect me to get married but you at least a little respect... cabbage rose one day and already I've replaced... or maybe you're just amused."

"Listen, please, Carla asked me only advice for the dissertation in medicine is going to support. Then, I don't hide that I brought back together but I was adamant, in fact I said I am in love and in that moment I crossed your terrified eyes... Oh, when I saw you run away

I broke the voice in my throat and I've chased ... please let me in the door, then I see you."

I stopped crying suddenly. A deaf and anger had strong possession of me. I would have gladly taken a slap.

"No. Don't open it. I will not live with a continuing threat sentimental. I don't want competitors in love."

A long silence. Rosa looked at me in obvious tension.

"Do as you like. I leave you time to think. Just know that I am here and that my feelings are the same as last night and this afternoon."

Unfortunately, even mine, but life has taught me to defend myself from possible pain. It's better to suffer now than when it's almost impossible to live away from him...

"If you need anything I'm here! Don't ever bother me, even at night..."

"Thank you Rosa. You are the friend who I always wanted."

It was Saturday morning and I had plenty of time to sleep. I sleep overshadowed and I was recurring the thought of the last few hours. I could not give me peace to the way that Giorgio had paid or for the unfortunate situation that we had arisen. Aware that the fault was no more than once because I put my trust in a man, I finally collapsed in a state of drowsiness. Salt and Pepper were squatting on my legs. I warmed more than one blanket. The bell had begun to play without stopping. Rosa could not say because I have a meeting at school. The alarm marked nine. I was half sleepy direct to the door and after looking through the peephole I almost felt I was missing. Alberto. God, but how did get my address? And why he had come up in Trentino? He was not yet for the time of Christmas holiday.

"Selvaggia, open please! I saw your car parked below. I know you're at home. "

More than a request seemed an order. Typical of his character. The scepter of command fascinated him in every situation.

"Hello! A fair wind brought you up to here? To not ask how the hell did you get my address."

I almost cried last phrase. I had alluded to enter, I didn't want to create scandal around the block. He was cold for the love of good clothes as usual he had tended to be practical. He wore leather shoes, ridiculous on snowy and a velvet jacket decidedly out of place to the place where he was. But to look beautiful he must suffer according to his mind! I was watching in my pajamas, wrapped in a pail full of childish doodles of a larger size and furry slippers shaped like a cat. If anyone had seen at that time, he would have defined the antithesis of each other. Yet I am not ashamed of my set, I was almost proud indeed. Now, far from Florence, I felt in control of my life. Alberto was a guest of a world hostile to him and certainly unknown. There were no nightclubs or popular super-equipped gyms. Where he was going to take his usual drink? And his luxurious dinner on Saturday night?

"Good welcome for a man who has done all these kilometers just to see you."

"Why you so upset? I never answered your phone calls and, when I went from Florence, I was clear about the permanent closure of our history."

I was furious. Then, suddenly, when I saw a slight desperation in her beautiful blue eyes, that I had a chance, last chance, you grant to anyone! Maybe I could tell by his closeness if which I was trying to Giorgio was just a crush or something really serious. How I wish it was just a stupid crush passing!

"In the bathroom there is a robe more, go to snag a hot shower that I prepare the breakfast. Talk later with more calm."

I didn't want to fall into the same routine for a moment, but I could not throw him away. I shared with him two years of my life. I could not forget him!

We did the breakfast in silence. Alberto at the end confessed to feeling alone without me and I understood how important I was for him. I don't think so, but I wanted to be consistent with myself and I see what he endured my current life. The mountain didn't leave his habits if he not for a quick winter holiday in a luxury hotel, even with a fully equipped beauty farm. I must not tell him because I would have taken as a challenge. He would have found alone. I, for myself, I already understood everything. Few words were enough to cause nausea. He was not wanted! And he still had some doubts at seeing was completely decayed. I loved him, but how you want it to friends. He was no longer for love. He wanted to stay with me forever. So he said this and I knew that he would not have survived for several days. I unsheathed my best smile and we went together in the small supermarket near you. We were choosing fruit when I heard a familiar voice behind me. A blow to the heart. I could not be him! Not now! I think that he is a fool who, after a tragedy for the appearance on the scene of his former girlfriend, you caught me in the company of the man who ruined her life. And everything to do displease him, a stupid revenge!

"Good morning Miss Mazzini."

"Hello, Doctor. How are you?"

Maybe she's after what had happened between us was like trying to distance. It hurt me to hear again a stranger to Giorgio. I could still linger with my wicker in hand. Alberto waited for me now.

"This is Mr. Pontini veterinarian of my cats. Alberto, my.... boyfriend."

I would rather run away and I attend to the accusatory gaze of Giorgio.

"Goodbye and I recommend you don't forget your check for Pepper in fifteen days. Pleasure to have known Alberto."

He had turned cold and hostile and he went directly to the cashier. I had lost. I wonder what he was thinking of me? A few nights ago I had vented my unfortunate love story, how I hated my old habits and the morning after our quarrel, I found her shopping at her company. A liar, he could only call me with this word!

Alberto brought with him the playstation. He turned on the television and, without asking the permission, he was thrown body and soul in those hateful childish games. I could not even read. The evening usually threw me on the couch, in the warmth of the fireplace, I opened my book to dream a bit open eyes. Salt and Pepper kept me company by playing with my slippers. Now those noises bothered me so much that I shut myself in the room. I felt a stranger in my house. Not to mention the only supper with Rosa, Tomas, Ines and Franz that he had openly snubbed. He barely even a smile right hateful when he discovered that the farmers did. How would born again that life far from any ease? I found a thousand excuses before I did sex with him. I was amazed of his stubbornness in wanting to stay. I spent more time outside and my afternoons were spent walking from one to two hours. Lounging on the couch and he said he would find a way to manage your work from afar. How can a lawyer working out of his study of competence? I was no longer going to yoga for fear of running into Giorgio and I didn't know anything about him because Rosa took care not to be alive. I understood that Alberto didn't feel her sympathy and she had left me the time to decide. Sometimes I waited at the door of the apartment building in overalls andI walked along the streets covered with snow. I listened without making judgments, just saying that I understand what my heart wants. I was sure that I no longer loved Alberto. His presence annoyed me, he had broken the balance that I had managed to acquire in those mountains. And I was sure that he was not due to my attraction to Giorgio, but my inner peace that vanished into thin air at his side. I loved that place and nothing in the world I returned to my beloved city, he could not live away from Florence.

"I talked to a realtor that I reviewed your apartment. We get a lot of money but we always manage to buy something in the suburbs."

I placed the fork on the plate to look at him straight in the eye. This was the moment of truth. Was required only one week.

"Alberto, you didn't understand anything! First of all you must not afford to take liberties that you are not granted because this house is mine, and the fruits of my labor. Then you have to put into my head that I will never leave this place. Never!

This is my heaven, I have tried it and I conquered it for the world forsake him!

Finally he took his things, including the odious playstation, and he went. I think that I was a thought removed also for Alberto. We were together for practice. After this sad and final attempt could let the matter rest. First I called Rosa and my others friends. I made pizza for all and after we had fun with a primary card game. Some evenings we went to the cinema to Bolzano and then stay to eat out. I was relieved but bitter. I have no longer time to find Giorgio after my yoga classes. I didn't know how. Pepper was completely healed and I was ashamed to introduce me to the clinic after I had seen with Alberto. I could not scold him if he had made on me the worst assumptions, including that of a good for nothing who pretend to be goody-goody. I had refused using my fear of being betrayed even before that something happened. And then he found me at the supermarket with my ex and so he much decried. What could I say in my defense? Any attempt to apologize would have been futile. He was a man of thirty years, with a mature and responsible job that he loved more than his own life. He could miss his time with a girl who had proved just immature? Within two days I gave myself for the worst. Not bad! On the one hand the work was proceeding at full speed because two other publishers in the province of Bolzano had sought me and I joined their staff as a single graphic. I had many things to do, but before I had to settle Ines and Franz who continued to ask a logo and a brochure for their new farm. These new friends have behaved discreetly. I have not spoken to Giorgio, knowing what had happened between us, or have opinions on Alberto (so that if they deserved). One morning in late November I was raised, and I nursed my bruised always ready to combine trouble, I had to walk directly to their farm. It was a huge house just outside the village. Painted white and with many balconies full of red cyclamen. In an adjacent barn, snowy lawn were three or four horses and two foals. I was told to have a small riding for guests. Ines I had received with his usual warm smile, and only after making me see some rooms, we were sitting in the large hall in front of a crackling fireplace. Franz had just reached us. I intent to write their requests on my calendar and I dont' realize if someone entered silently.

"The horses enjoy good health, you just keep them as warm. The outside temperature is too low for them."

Giorgio was standing in the doorway and he was watching Franz and I was openly ignored. My heart sank and I had blocked out and I could not write anymore. My legs were trembling with shame. Ines was raised to me was left there alone on that sofa too big where I seemed to sink.

"I'm going to prepare two hot chocolate! Giorgio sit down and you say because you know that you owe me... then sit by the fire and not a word."

Having said that, he removed to the kitchen in the company of Franz. At that moment I was certain that there was the hand of Rosa in this "accidental" meeting. How would I do without them? Who would make me such a surprise of my "friends" of the past?

"How's Pepper?"

"Very well, thank you. He runs faster than before."

He smiled and quickly he turned his eyes to the flames of fire, for better or want me to avoid punishment.

"I'm sorry. I was a fool in the fluid that way this Friday night... I was afraid that you might reconsider and decide to go with that girl... Carla, I think you call it... I'm sorry if you can."

I had a weak voice and a little courage, but in front of me was the only man who I could love. He had my own passions, loved the place in which he lived was so beautiful and breathtaking. He wore a checkered shirt and trousers pail velvet blacks, keeping unusual work.

"You are insecure by nature and you tend not to trust in others. I don't think you owe me an apology. Maybe you should make them your boyfriend saw what happened between us."

He was cold and unfriendly. I was helping and I could not scold him, I find the strength to tell him how important he was for me.

"There is no boyfriend! The situation is the same as I told you that night. Then he introduced himself to my house unannounced and I did not felt to throw off the street saw many kilometers. And I say that was the most important experience of my life because I was certain not to love him and perhaps he had never loved. I had linked to him because of my insecurities that this place has started to heal. In the long weeks fortunately he felt that he would never work, we are the one opposite the other."

"Why do you say that?"

Now he was challenging his eyes. I had chills all over my body but I tried to appear calm and determined.

"Because I think I'm ready to not be afraid. Ie to have no fears about you and who can life with you. I can take this risk and, if he not work, he will be more painful longing I felt in all these nights when coming out of my yoga class I have never managed to bump into you. I missed the earth beneath my feet and I thought I'd never had the opportunity to explain everything, to apologize for my childish behavior and what I want to tell you. No man can ever take your place in my heart. You are half full to me and he gives me the strength to face every daily problem."

"You could come to my office. Pepper had to do to control or am I wrong?"

I was holding back her tears but surely my eyes were red and shiny. Because it is harder than I thought? Because I was so hasty in judging that evening?

"And if you do you had better be accepted or you had spent my visit to another vet?"

"See, Selvaggia, the peace that gave me this place has also made me realize that nothing is as it seems. I could not judge you by your side because you saw Alberto. And I would just reviewed by one. So I understand if you told me a lie. But you, a coward, you never submitted to my office."

Rosa and Franz didn't arrive, something told me that they were waiting for the end of the debate and I would not surprised if I'd accompany them through the door to listen.

"That means that you don't give me another chance?"

"How could I not give it to you? I thought about you every moment and I hope that Alberto had gone. I avoided going to the sauna at the times when there were yoga classes. I wanted you to analyze your heart. And if this is the result of well-being. I'm here!"

I never thought a moment and I launched the agenda on the table, I had thrown in his arms.

"Hot chocolate with whipped cream!"

Franz, Inez, Tomas and Rosa were fun watching us. Their plan had the desired effect. The great Shakespeare was right when he said that "nothing is right or wrong but it is the mind that makes it so." Before you make judgments now we will think about it! It's harder to be forgiven than to be loved.

Salt and Pepper were so happy to have Giorgio always around and they doesn't leave him alone even when he went to shower. Patients they were waiting outside the bathroom door. At first I almost felt jealous then I realized that was their only way for me to understand that shared my choice. The day before we went to the Christmas market in Bressanone and, as always, I became fascinated by the small-town gem. The town looked like a village in the tie, colorful, orderly and very clean. The stands were full of colorful glass beads, fabric or china. The main square was crowded. Snowing incessantly, but we were still able to buy more decorations than we would be served. Giorgio had not reckoned with our pests playing with the balls that we should stick to our Christmas tree. I was in seventh heaven about how things were going between us. After our explanation, my handsome veterinarian had moved into my flat, we were a couple now in effect! We had fun cooking together. I became good at dumplings and sweet crepes are typical of these mountains. Rosa, Franz, Ines and Tomas were our guinea pigs. Every Saturday we organize a challenge with some cards or board games. In the evening we relaxed on the couch to watch a movie or just to keep us company while everyone was reading your book. Plato was right. There is only one person in the world with which we can feel truly realized.

December 29, 2008

This is my story. Nothing special just the example of how our lives can change with our choices. Remain basking on their mistakes and wallow in endless pain circuits. I don't know if Giorgio is the man of my life (I hope so) because I stopped asking and I learned to live day by day. What I have today tomorrow will be just a sweet memory, ultimately we smile even on the pain passed when they no longer have power to hurt us. Here I found the inner peace regardless of the man who lives next to me. I reassessed my person and I have accepted my way of being or ceasing to find inadequate to deal with others. I am so, with my faults but also with my merits and they are many. I finally tasted the flavor of true friendship, who isn't contaminated by envy or by resentment, I can rely on this friendship in every moment of my life. I don't know what stress is and I enjoy every moment of my day. In short, I never want to be from other parts of the world if not here and I thank Alberto for having hurt, humiliated and driven to make a change so drastic that it has been a great revival!

Selvaggia

Christmas market in the city of Bressanone

http://www.bressanone.it/

web page of the little village where i set the history of Selvaggia: COLLALBO

http://www.suedtirol-it.com/renon/collalbo.htm

Summer landscape in the Valle of Renon

Winter landscape in Val di Non

www.samilla.wordpress.com

www.catastinisamanta.ilcannocchiale.it

www.italianromances.wordpress.com

www.ingramcontent.com/pod-product-compliance
Ingram Content Group UK Ltd.
Pitfield, Milton Keynes, MK11 3LW, UK
UKHW020233250726
13967UKWH00001B/347

9 781446 157084